THE HEART OF A WHALE

Anna Pignataro

For Rebecca Young.

And also for Mark, with all my heart.

And for Isabella, whose song is so beautiful
it can reach the farthest of faraways.

PHILOMEL BOOKS
An imprint of Penguin Random House LLC, New York

First published in Australia by Scholastic Press in 2018.
First published in the United States of America by Philomel,
an imprint of Penguin Random House LLC, 2020.

Visit us online at penguinrandomhouse.com

LIBRARY OF CONGRESS CATALOGING-IN-PUBLICATION DATA
Names: Pignataro, Anna, author, illustrator. Title: The heart of a whale / Anna Pignataro.
Description: New York : Philomel Books, 2020. | "First published in Australia by Scholastic Press in 2018." | Summary: Whale's
beautiful song calms a wriggly octopus, cheers a sad urchin, and much more but cannot cure his loneliness without the help
of his friends. | Identifiers: LCCN 2019018656 | ISBN 9781984836274 (hardcover) | ISBN 9781984836298 (e-book) | ISBN 9781984836281
(e-book) | Subjects: | CYAC: Whales—Fiction. | Marine animals—Fiction. | Loneliness—Fiction. | Whale sounds—Fiction.
Classification: LCC PZ7.P62517 He 2020 | DDC [E]—dc23 LC record available at https://lccn.loc.gov/2019018656

Manufactured in China

ISBN 9781984836274

10 9 8 7 6 5 4 3 2 1

Edited by Talia Benamy. Original design by Sarah Mitchell. This edition designed by Jennifer Chung. Text set in AskesHandwriting.

THE HEART OF A WHALE

Anna Pignataro

Philomel Books

Whale's song was so beautiful
it could reach the farthest of faraways.

It sang of happiness and hope,
magic and wonder,
    always and everywhere.

It was a calming sonata
   for a wriggly octopus.

   A cheerful symphony
      for a sad urchin.

An orchestra for a ballet of ocean flowers.

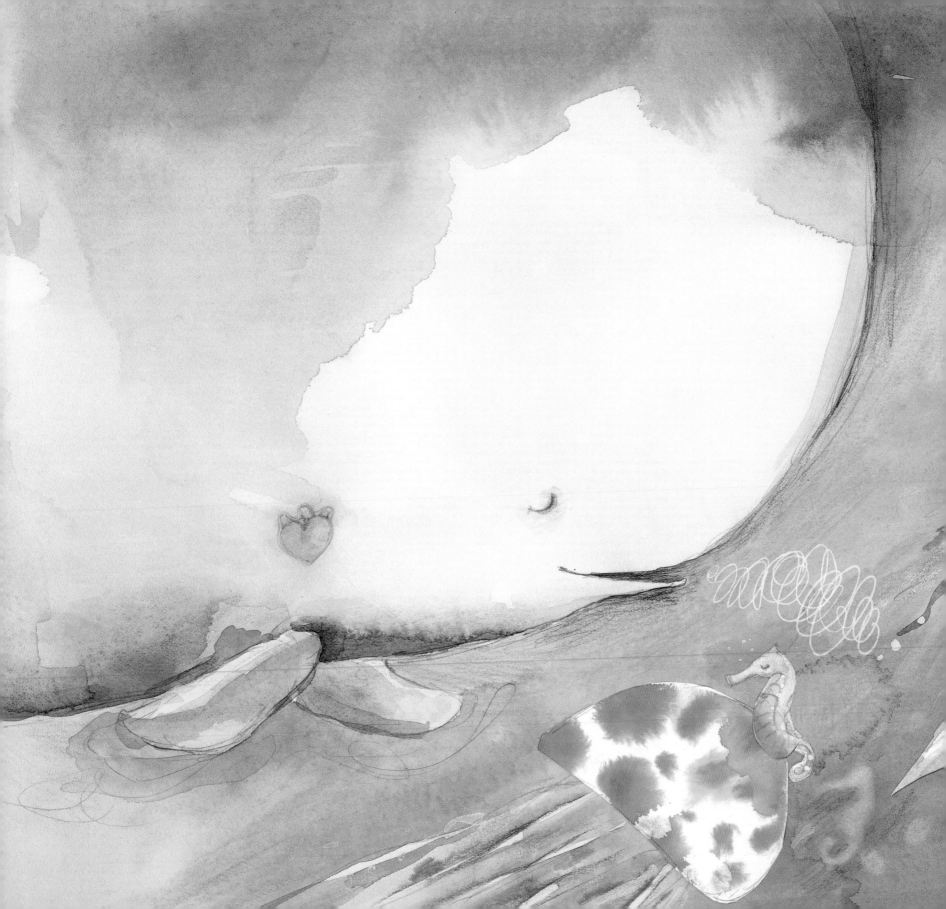

A lullaby for a herd
of newborn seahorses.

Whale sang day after day,
   night after night,
      warmly weaving a path of starlight
         into the seagrass taller than a forest . . .

and through the wild and
tangled undergrowth.

But even with the roaring waves above him,
    even with the pounding drumbeat of his heart,
        even with his song . . .

Whale thought how quiet
        the sea could be at times . . .

and how there was no song big enough
to fill his empty heart.

Whale sighed.

His sigh drifted away like a wish.

A wish that the ocean carefully gathered
and carried for him.

Past seabeds,
  through fathoms,

       over dreaming turtles
       and forgotten treasure . . .

to another

who followed the wish

through the sea . . .

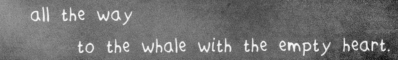

all the way
to the whale with the empty heart.

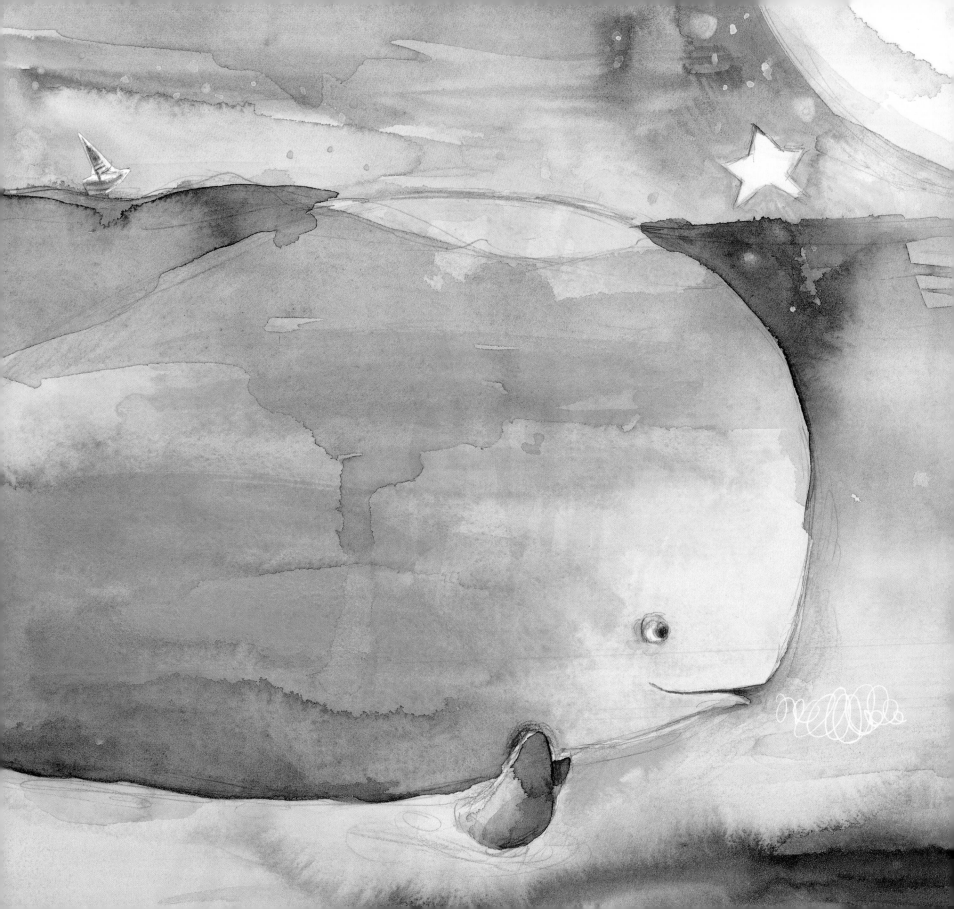

Together they sang
of happiness and hope,
magic and wonder . . .

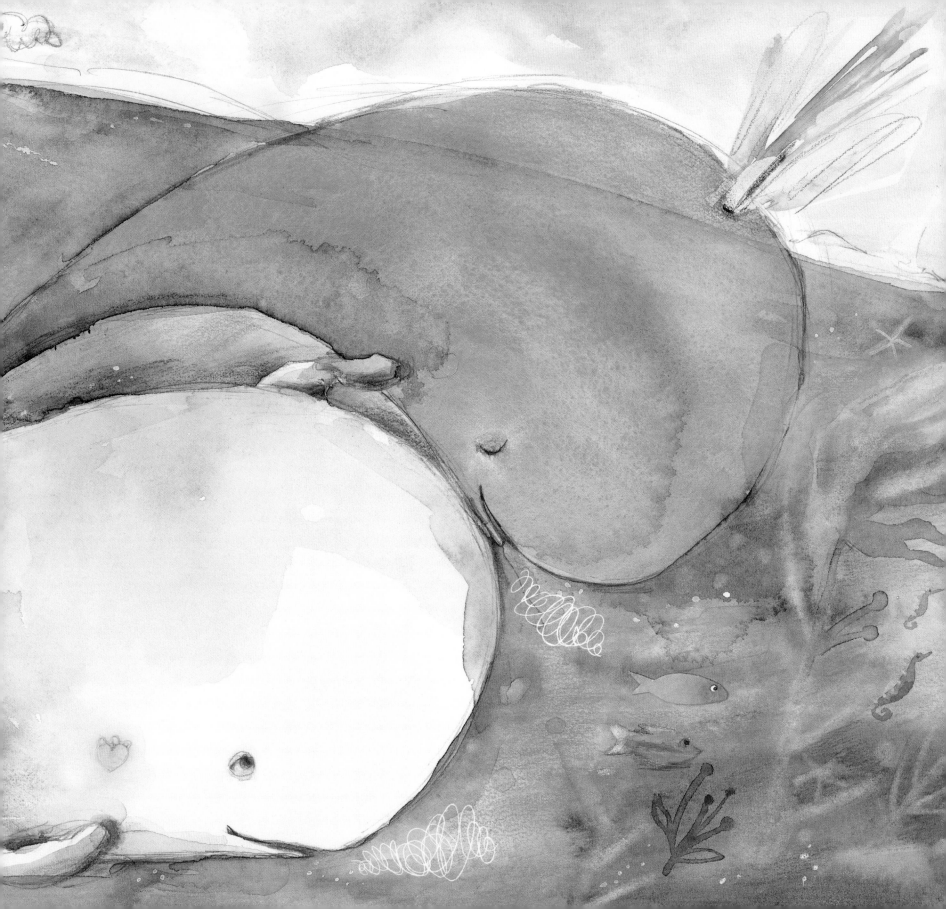

always

and

everywhere.